the Littlest Angel meets the Newest Angel

By
Ronald Kidd

Illustrated
by
Rick Reinert

Ideals Publishing
Nashville, Tennessee

Copyright © MCMLXXXVI by Childrens Press

ISBN 0-8249-8077-8

It was Monday morning in the Kingdom of Heaven, and for the Littlest Angel that meant just one thing: a visit with his friend the Gatekeeper. It was the Littlest Angel's favorite time of the week, a time when he and the Gatekeeper could walk or talk or play hide-and-seek in the clouds, just the two of them.

This Monday it was hide-and-seek, and as usual the Gatekeeper was losing. He might have been a good player except for two things: when hiding he tended to stand up and wave to passersby, and when seeking he nodded off to sleep. The Littlest Angel didn't mind, though, because he loved the kindly Gatekeeper and enjoyed spending time with him.

The Littlest Angel was just coming out from a hiding place to wake up his friend for the third time, when he heard the sound of chimes.

The Gatekeeper's eyes flew open. "The gate!" he said. "We have a new arrival!" He struggled to his feet and straightened his halo. "I'm coming!" he called.

"What about our game?" asked the Littlest Angel. "We're not finished yet."

"Don't worry," said the Gatekeeper, "I'll be right back." And with that, he hurried off.

The Littlest Angel did a few halfhearted somersaults, then sat down to wait. After waiting for an hour, he grew impatient and made his way to the Heavenly Gate, where his friend stood talking to someone.

"Are you finished yet?" asked the Littlest Angel.

The Gatekeeper turned around. "Oh, my goodness," he said, "in the excitement I forgot all about you."

"Excitement?"

The Gatekeeper nodded eagerly. "Littlest Angel," he said, "meet the Newest Angel."

He stepped aside to reveal a blonde-haired cherub barely taller than the Littlest Angel. Her eyes shone, and her skin was as smooth and white as the pearly gate itself.

The Littlest Angel turned to the Gatekeeper. "Can you come back and play with me now?"

"I'd like to," he replied, "but I need to show the Newest Angel around Paradise. Want to come along?"

"No, thanks," mumbled the Littlest Angel.

The Gatekeeper nodded understandingly, then he took the Newest Angel's hand and led her away.

Disappointed, the Littlest Angel decided to
go visit one of his other friends, the Wingmaker.
He found the plump, curly-haired angel lying
on her stomach in front of her house peering
down through the mist.

"What are you doing?" the Littlest Angel
asked her.

"Watching clouds," she answered. "Come
on down and have a look."

He flopped down beside her and gazed
earthward. Below them, clouds floated across
the face of the earth like puffy white boats.

"That one looks like an elephant," said the
Wingmaker, "with a trunk and two big ears.
Can you see it?"

The Littlest Angel nodded and pointed at
some other clouds. "There's a bunny rabbit and
a house. And a bear standing on its head."

The Wingmaker giggled. "I see a doughnut without a hole. Or maybe it's a hole without a doughnut."

"Those two little clouds across the way look like angels," said the small cherub.

"Why, they are angels," said the Wing-maker, "and they're coming this way! It's the Gatekeeper . . . but who's that with him?"

The Littlest Angel saw a small, familiar figure with blonde hair walking next to the Gatekeeper. "Nobody important," he said quickly. Peering back down below, he cried, "Look, that cloud's shaped like a dinosaur!"

But the Wingmaker didn't hear him. She was already hurrying forward to meet her visitors. The Littlest Angel watched as she leaned down and gave the new arrival a big hug. Without waiting for the Wingmaker to return, the Littlest Angel stomped off.

He moped around for the rest of the morning, going no place in particular. By early afternoon he found himself in the Celestial City. There, just like everywhere else in Heaven, the crowds were buzzing about the Newest Angel.

"She's as lovely as a lily in bloom," they were saying. "She has rosy cheeks and a sparkle in her eye, and when she smiles, all Heaven lights up."

It wasn't so long ago, thought the Littlest Angel, that it was me everyone was talking about. Well, maybe I can make them talk about me again.

He ran along the Street of Guardian Angels, shouting at the top of his lungs. He jumped into the Fountain of Eternal Life and did the backstroke. He flew high above the trees, then swooped down on the Heavenly Host, making sounds like a crow. He did all the things that usually got him attention and lots of it.

The angels barely even noticed.

Then one of the Patriarch Prophets saw
him and pointed. "Look who's here!" he cried,
hurrying toward the Littlest Angel.

The small cherub stood tall, his tiny chest
swelling with pride.

As the prophet drew near, he slowed down and came to a halt. "Whoops, my mistake," he said, straightening his spectacles. "I thought you were the Newest Angel."

The Littlest Angel trudged out of the Celestial City, his wings drooping, and headed for the Elysian Fields. He had spent many happy days there since arriving in Heaven, with the birds and flowers and trees as his only

playmates. During that time, he had come to
think of the fields as his home.

He lay down in his favorite meadow and
stared up at the sky, thinking how nice Heaven
used to be before the Newest Angel had arrived.

Just then, there were footsteps and the sound of voices. He sat up and saw the Gatekeeper and the Newest Angel approaching.

Jumping to his feet, he demanded, "What's she doing here?"

"I thought this might be a good place for her to live," replied the Gatekeeper.

The Littlest Angel could hardly believe his ears. "But it's already full," he said.

"Oh," said the Gatekeeper, with a twinkle in his eye, "I think there might be room for one more. Now be an angel and show your new neighbor around. I need to be going." He gave them both a pat on the halo and left.

The Littlest Angel turned to the Newest Angel. "Well," he mumbled, "I suppose you could stay on the far side of the fields, over there. *Way* over there."

The Newest Angel looked at the ground and nodded.

He led her through the meadow and across a stream to a remote corner of the fields.

"Okay," he said, "here's your place. Just remember, stay on this side of the stream. Everything on the other side belongs to me."

Leaving her there, he crossed the stream and went back. He spent the rest of the day chasing butterflies and rolling in the grass. Later that night, as he lay in the meadow gazing down at the stars, he thought of a plan.

The Littlest Angel woke up early the next morning. He borrowed tools from the Halosmith and went into the woods to chop down some trees. He cut them into posts and used them to build a fence around his part of the fields. Then he put a sign on the fence which said:

PROPERTY OF
THE LITTLEST ANGEL
KEEP OUT

To make sure everyone obeyed, he spent his days patrolling the fence. In fact, he spent so much time patrolling that he hardly had any time to play. But he didn't mind, because it meant that once again he had something that was all his own.

A week went by, then another. And then while on patrol one day, he heard music and laughter coming from the other side of the fence. He peeked over the top of the fence, and across the stream he saw the Gatekeeper and Wingmaker with their arms linked, dancing a jig. Nearby, the Singer (also known as the Understanding Angel) was plucking a harp and raising his voice in song. Next to him, the Newest Angel was giggling and clapping her hands.

The Littlest Angel turned away and resumed his patrol, determined to ignore the sounds. But the long, lonely days had taken their toll. Each time around, the laughter seemed louder and the music more cheerful.

Finally he couldn't stand it anymore. He squeezed through the gate and jumped over the stream. As he approached the happy group, the Gatekeeper broke into a wide grin and waved.

The Littlest Angel joined them, at first standing quietly next to the Singer. Soon, though, he found himself tapping his foot and humming along. As he did, he noticed something strange. He had given the Newest Angel

only a small corner of the Elysian Fields and kept the rest for himself. And yet at that moment, her corner, brimming with life, seemed bigger than all the vast empty spaces of his own fenced domain.

He felt a hand on his shoulder, and he turned to see the Newest Angel smiling and holding out her hand. She pulled him into the clearing, where they began to dance their own youthful version of the jig. A moment later they

joined hands with the Gatekeeper and Wingmaker. The four of them spun, slowly at first,
then faster and faster, forming a circle as warm
and golden as the halos they wore.

The Newest Angel smiled at him, and all at once the Littlest Angel knew just what he wanted to do. He let go of their hands and ran out of the clearing. Leaping across the stream, he headed straight for his fence. With two quick motions, he tore down the sign and threw open the big wooden gate.

"Come on in," called the Littlest Angel.
"There's plenty of room!"
They did. And there was.

And ever since that day, the Littlest Angel and the Newest Angel have been the closest of friends, living as neighbors in a corner of Heaven where fences are forbidden, and the only signs are those that say welcome.